THE DAY TAJON GOT SHOT

BY THE TEEN WRITERS OF BEACON HOUSE

T'ASIA, J'YONA, REIYANNA, JONAE, MAKIYA, ROSE, NAJAE, SERENITY, JEANET, AND TEMIL

SHOUT**MOUSE**
PRESS

A Shout Mouse Press Production
in collaboration with
Shootback and Beacon House

Washington, DC | 2017

Beacon House / Shout Mouse Press

Published by
Shout Mouse Press, Inc.
www.shoutmousepress.org

Copyright © 2017 Shout Mouse Press, Inc.
ISBN-13: 978-0996927451
ISBN-10: 099692745X

Book design by Heather Butterfield and Zoe Gatti.

PHOTOGRAPHS / ARTWORK
The Black Lives Matter cover photograph was licensed under a Creative Commons Attribution License by Fibonacci Blue, November 15, 2015, Minnesota. Adapted by Zoe Gatti.

The following photographs were taken by teen authors or Lana Wong and produced in collaboration with the Shootback Project: pages xiii, xiv-xxvii, 6, 11, 15, 20, 22-23, 28, 44, 53, 70, 73, 77, 87, 89, 90, 97, 115, 119, 123, 152-153, 174, 176-177, 180-189.

Unless otherwise noted, all photographs of real-world protests and riots were taken by Amir Price, a DC-based teen photographer, during the Baltimore uprising of April 2015: pages 36-40, 56-57, 126-127, 130-132, copyright © Amir Price. Learn more: criticalexposure.org/news-and-events/press

All original artwork was produced by teen authors and attributed whenever possible. Back cover artwork by Serenity Summers.